Remember Me Tomorrow

A Novella

By Christopher A Griffin

Printed in the United States of America

First Printing, 2020

EPUB ISBN 978-1-7329377-3-4

PRINT ISBN 978-1-7329377-2-7

Edited by Richard Arcus

Cover Art by Andrew Forteath

Chapter One

November 2nd, 2020
3:15 AM
I am a forgetful man. All that was before, is now
gone.

November 2nd, 2020
11:08 PM
I must write this down, for tomorrow it may be too
late. I must immortalize these thoughts.

Today I found myself in an open window high above the city street, poised to step out of it into the open morning air. I don't recall anything before that moment. Thinking on it now, I should have been more scared than I was. Before writing these words I was thinking of how fearful I must have been, but upon reflection now I feel it must have happened before. To write that this was the first time this has occurred, feels like a lie.

There are pages missing from this journal. Many pages have been torn out. You should know, I don't remember things, or people, places. I try to keep a record of each day's events, otherwise life would be a near impossibility.

Back to today. I remember voices coming up at me from below. Many voices, I don't remember specifically what anyone was saying. It didn't matter. I must have had a reason for being in that window. I remember now, I did want to die.

There it is, that familiar cold feeling. I was angry about something. I remember, I was angry at the world. I don't remember if I was yelling back at the faceless people below ,or if it was only in my mind, but a ferocity brewed within me: one that erupted in that moment, and only in that moment did I finally get to articulate what had plagued me all my life. Which was that life, that meaning itself, had betrayed me. The very root of humanity, the core of what we are here to do, is to discover and declare our identity. To bring order to our own personal slice of chaos. But, that process, that privilege of everyone else, had been denied to me.

I don't know if I had been robbed of it my whole life, or only the last stretch of time until that moment today. I envied them, I hated them. I still hate them now. Even in this moment I loathe everyone else.

know that, standing in that window, I had every intention to step off that ledge, to surrender myself to oblivion, to give in, to give up all that I had, which was nothing.

There was a woman. Yes, I remember now, there was a woman behind me in the room. She spoke to me. I hadn't known she was there. I don't know how long she had been there, and I hadn't heard her come in. Her voice was soft, and it stifled the sounds of chaos in my mind. She asked what I was doing, but I couldn't answer. I tried desperately at that moment for any response that would justify absolutely anything about that situation, but nothing surfaced. I remember asking her who she was.

She replied that she was my wife.

The horror of that thought. I had, HAVE a wife? I can picture her face as she stood there watching me. She was beautiful. Her hair was brown, or blonde. Already she is starting to fade.

Was she telling the truth? Now, I'm not so sure. Who would marry me, with all my faults, my handicaps? To marry me would be to fall into my trap, my con. It would be a cruel gesture to con someone into marrying me. That's the only way I can describe it. I must have made her feel so hopeless, if she even was my wife.

She showed me a picture of her and a man. She was in a wedding dress. The man looked like me. I remember thinking that in that moment, but now I'm not so sure. I hadn't looked at myself today. What do I look like? Am I unattractive? She told me a story of how we met. As she spoke I studied her face for any hint or trace of recollection I could find. I don't know why I was so fixated on that. I think I was trying to catch her in a lie, or perhaps hoping for a glimmer, a spark, of a memory.

The memories are there, somewhere amongst the catacombs of the past. I often feel as though I am in a dark library. The books line the shelves, but have no labels, no order. Even when I find the memory I have been searching for, once it's placed back upon the shelf there is no way of knowing if or when I will find it again.

Back to the window. I'm thinking now, whether it was reason or a desire that put me in that window earlier today. I know in the first moment I remember from this morning, I wanted to jump. Just in that briefest, tiniest, fraction of a second, I was ready. I could feel the faint exquisite pleasure of acceptance. But my hands never let go of the frame.

The thought loosely occurred to me then, but I don't think I fully understood it until now. Reason and desire. Which comes first, is there an order? Do you need a reason first to desire to degrade yourself, to freefall into the blackness of thought towards self-destruction? Or is it the other way around. Do you desire to recede from the world and then find existence itself the reason to shrink away?

The path to redemption is even harder to see. I don't think desire can come first. When you're in that dark place already, when there is no light, and surrender is the only thing that remains. You need a reason first to move upward. Harder still I think is that you need maybe not one reason to ascend, but many.

Perhaps it was some unknowable, unconscious slice of a reason that kept my hands in place today.

Maybe the woman was telling the truth. I felt more sure that she probably was. I have a wife.

Although this revelation led to a flurry of questions, my lips remained locked. Asking a question would risk learning an answer I may not have wanted to hear. Asking a question would risk that familiar cold feeling, losing that slim glimmer keeping me on that ledge. To not know, was the bliss I could find.

Her hand wrapped around me effortlessly, pulling me back into the room. Cheering voices rose from the street outside, out the window. I wondered whether my averting death was truly a victory. Perhaps the cheers were for themselves; that the tragedy before them was over, and they could return to their own perhaps-mediocre lives free of guilt and sadness. My envy for them returned briefly.

I found myself facing the woman who said she was my wife. How alien the moment felt. She was so beautiful, but I was momentarily immobilized in my speech. I managed to thank her for pulling me back, but my words were forced. Nothing lay behind them. The words tasted a lie in my mouth. She stared at me silently.

The door burst open. People filled the room as I thought to myself. Police, paramedics, more police. An endless flood of uniforms moved in an orchestrated dance. I remember not one person made eye contact with me as I found myself surrounded by strangers.

A cop pulled my hands behind my back and placed cuffs on me. The woman yelled louder and louder at them, pleading that I had done nothing wrong.

I think I did do something wrong, as I think on it now. I must have. I'm not religious, but I know I must have sinned. After all, to sin is to miss your mark. And that's what I did, I missed my mark catastrophically. But I realize now, I know that I missed. Isn't that the first step, to know when you missed something, to know that you're off target?

There is a power in knowing that a wrong was committed. It is a difficult truth that must be confronted, but not just directly, it must be integrated. It must be folded into oneself. It must be draped over one's shoulders and carried from then on until it isn't needed anymore. I feel crippled by the sheer weight, which is at a near-unbearable level. Perhaps that is the reason I found myself where I was.

The cuffs were tight. The steel was cold, I remember. The woman hugged me as the cop tried to pull her away. Remember, she said. I can still hear those words in my head even now. How soft her words were. How gentle. I remember a flash came to me, of her in the rain. She was laughing. We were happy. The flash went away, back to nothingness.

The cop pulled her away as paramedics closed in. A thousand questions they asked. How do you feel, are you ok, I remember them asking in between all the technical questions. The answer seemed evident enough for me. One medic said I was ok, and just as quickly the cop began moving me towards the door. It was the first time I had really looked around the room. It was almost completely empty, save for a chair, some books, and a small TV on the floor.

I realize now, I'm not writing this in that same place. How I got here evades me. This room is dark. Voices murmur through the floor. It will come to me. Back to earlier today. I must get this down before I forget the importance of it all.

In the hall, people were staring. The looks on their faces varied. Some looked on pitifully, others looked with shame, with judgement. The word sin popped in my mind again. No, it was a sin to kill yourself, which is not what I did. I didn't do it. I could have, I should have. It's her fault. The woman. My wife.

No. It can't be, it's not her fault. How could I put that on someone, anyone, especially someone I'm supposed to love, to care for.

It's me. I did this. I drove myself to this. I, me, not you, not her, me, I, that's who did it. I hate writing this, but it's true. Maybe I didn't step off the window ledge, but must have stepped off a ledge of some sort to arrive here. I was ready to do it. I was. It was in me, the strength, or the cowardice. Which one, I don't know, but one of them is true. But I was saved by her. My wife.

Her name, I didn't think of it then, but I do now. It's there, her name. Burned on my mind like a cattle brand. Ariadne.

I remember her name.

Ariadne was behind me as the officer escorted me down the winding steps of the apartment building. He didn't say a word as we descended.

In my mind I screamed my story to tell the people as I passed. I begged for forgiveness, for punishment. Anything I could to satiate my desire to not only be heard, but to have a purpose, or at least a perception of one.

Reality returned as we exited the building out on to the city street. A silence seemed to have befallen the crowd, as everyone stared in amazement. They must have thought of me as loathsome, a despicable excuse for a man. The pity of a dozen judgmental sets of eyes penetrated my very soul. A hand touched my back gently. It was Ariadne. She must have sensed my vulnerability. The feeling that she was in fact my wife was proven utterly and completely true in that moment. I yearned to redo the day, make different choices. But a cold shiver came back at the thought. I don't know what led me to that ledge. So how could I know, or even attempt to claim to know, how to avoid it. Destiny met me on that window ledge today. It changed me incontrovertibly. I felt it in my very bones.

Before I knew it, I was led to a police car. The door was open. A man in the crowd was clapping solemnly at me. I don't know what was meant by this. The sight distracted me from Ariadne moving in front. She said something softly. I can't remember now what she said. There was a sadness in her expression. She looked at me through tear-filled eyes. She kissed me gently. The memory came back, of her in the rain. I think she said she loved me. Even now, I'm not sure.

In that moment, I knew why I was on that ledge. Now, it is so clear, so tangible I can almost touch the reason. It exists, it's real, and I can see it now. I was there for her to save me.

Yes, yes that is the reason. I did want to die, at first, but there was something else, something deeper beneath the pain. It was a desire to be reached, rescued. By her, my wife. At least, that seems like what I think. I thought I had it, just then. I was so close. Perhaps I couldn't write it fast enough. It was right there, but now it's blurred.

At least I know a truth now that I didn't before. The truth is that now I don't want to die.

Chapter Two

October 10th, 2004

I fear I am losing my mind. What grip I had on reality is slowly slipping away. I can feel it, even as I write this. The rug has been moved gently beneath the feet that are my life. Part of me struggled against it for years, but another part of me egged it to move more swiftly.

What is it to lose your mind? Society defines it in so many subtle and excruciatingly tedious ways. For me, it started slowly; forgetting a name, or a place. Occasionally I'd lose my train of thought or use the wrong word. Most of the time I could explain it away. Lack of sleep, drank too much, stress, etc. How the lies came more and more easily. Only this journal knows the true extent of them. Sometimes the lie would write itself, and I would deliver it obediently. There are days when I feel everyone is in on some kind of joke but me. Yet, some days, no one is in on it all: because, in truth, there is no joke. On those occasions whole days or weeks can become lost. Erased from time. The depths and boundaries of my isolation are complete, and no amount of force can bring me out of it.

I forgot to pick up the kids today. It had been a whole year since the last instance. Ariadne was furious with me. Our lives were so regimented, so many notes, reminders, alarms. I'm not sure what happened. I arrived home three hours late. She asked if I had been at work. That was an instance where time was lost. Why does time move differently for me than everyone else? Funny thing, time is. It is a privilege for the sane; only the insane get to enjoy its ignorance.

The kids still don't know, how could they? How do you explain memory loss to elementary school children? Ariadne knows she has to tell them someday. A mother should not have to tell her kids their dad is losing his memory and mind.

Worse atrocities have befallen men, I suppose. Countless millions have died at the hands of governments, dictators. Society can begrudge itself one poor man with no memory. Alzheimer's, the doctor calls it. Slow to take, slow to feel its work.

So subtle it started, years ago. A million centuries of evolution feels more apt. I imagine it starts in a way most people can relate as I would suspect. I would get in the car to go to work and wake up in the parking lot of the office. My commute was an hour most days. I would try desperately to recollect the route, but nothing would surface. My thoughts would turn dark with possibilities.

It's horrid; so horrid I dare not think of it, even now. Eventually my license was revoked after a near accident. Ariadne did all the driving after that, it was obvious the kids became aware of something. Work became an increasing struggle too as the amount of notes needed to manage the day grew exponentially. It worsened as time went on.

Days blurred together, then weeks, months, seasons, years. Years. Saying it, even all these years on, sickens me. It is easy to lose oneself thinking of how you treated people, what you accomplished throughout that time. Just so I can say that I am alive? I don't feel I have much to show for surviving all that time. I can't imagine what was I like, especially to Ariadne through the years. I may as well had been a zombie, barely speaking, perhaps spoke differently, or even at all.

I should feel guilty. I don't feel guilty now. I hate myself for not feeling guilty. But for what reason should I feel this way. If I was kind all this time I should feel grateful, but a reason is lacking for that as well. How am I to feel anything except, empty. Soulless. How contemptible.

I remember Ariadne screamed at me today for forgetting about the kids. She said after the last time that it could never happen again. She said she loathed me, the very sight of me, in that moment. I could tell she was on the brink of an eruption that was rightly deserved. I remained silent.

She said she resented me so much she sometimes wished we hadn't met.

The revelation struck me in a way I hadn't anticipated. It wasn't frustration, or sadness, it was release. Yes, that's what it was. I racked my brain to describe it. A weight had been lifted off my shoulders.

The words paralyzed her after they came out. I loved her in that moment more than any other time I could recall. I loved her, not because I knew she didn't mean it, but because she did. It was a moment of honesty that set her free of this hellish nightmare I have imprisoned her in. It was catharsis for her, and I could never deny her that.

I moved toward Ariadne and held out my arms. She fell into me, sobbing. She gripped my body and screamed into my chest, her weight heavy in my arms. Neither of us said a word, but our embrace was filled with a new kind of love we hadn't previously discovered.

I remember our first date. She sat across from me in a booth in a diner. She had a tie in her hair that was bright purple. I don't know why that sticks out. She twirled her fork on the plate like she was eating spaghetti dozens of times throughout the meal. Such tiny details override everything else. She stared at me over the table, practically through me. We understood each other. We needed each other. As we do now.

I don't know how long we remained there; maybe minutes, maybe hours. I lost track. Sometime later she pulled away, her makeup running down her cheek.

Her apology came in a small, subdued voice. She raised her hand, cupped my face, and asked me what it was like to lose memories sometimes as fast as they formed. Still, I remained silent. She knew someday I would forget not just this outburst, but possibly her entirely. The thought sent shivers down my spine. She was my everything. I still remember how we met.

It's gone now, for a brief second it was there, the image, but now the image is gone. If I reread this section again then maybe the memory will return. Ariadne, if you ever read this, please do not judge me for the sin of losing one of the most coveted memories I possess.

I don't know if anyone will ever read this. Maybe I will dare to glance at these pages again in the future.

The point is this, continuity. I must maintain, I must endure beyond this moment.

For all I am is the present. I have no past, as I seemingly have no future. I do not mean that in the literal sense. I, of course, technically, will have a future, but how am I to take aim at any goal knowing full well I may never hit my mark. Imagine firing arrows out into the night sky, completely and ignorantly unaware of any ever striking anything, even the ground. Then of what use is it to continue to take aim? But still I do. I am obliged to. Not to myself, of course. It is useless to try to appeal to myself any further. No, I am obliged to someone else, anyone else really. Ariadne, I am obliged to her. The truth is that I am becoming afraid of the future. Afraid that I no longer will know where the truth ends and my illusions of truth begin.

What is the last true thing I remember? I am alive, I know that, I breathe, I think, I feel.

Deeper than superficial truths lies the one thing the triumphs over the creeping doubts, it's that I am not alone. Ariadne exists. She is real. My kids are real, though I fear their names have already escaped me.

I must confess my pen left the page for a considerable amount of time after writing that last sentence. I cannot remember the names of my own children, and, instead of searching for their names, all that filled me was a desire for tomorrow. I knew why, but didn't want to say. I will write it now to make permanent my evil thoughts. Because by tomorrow I likely will not even remember that I have children, and it would save me from the indignity, the shamefulness, the cruelty of forgetting their names in the first place. I fear I have hit rock bottom. I'd rather be a forgetful fool, than a horrific abominable father and husband. Better to be hapless than try to convince everyone that it wasn't out of taking my family for granted. I don't do this to save myself any grace or pride, but to spare the ones I love from pity. To you reading this, I am not a martyr, don't make that mistake. I am cowardly, I deserve cruelty. I condemn myself, I have condemned myself. The darkness within me has looked at me, and held out its hand. I fear I don't have much reason to keep my hand idle any longer.

After a time I dared to ask Ariadne about the children. I remember I asked their names. Even now, the truth evades me. Sometimes I don't know if I actually forget details or if my own subconscious chooses to forget. The vileness is the same either way.

She told me about them. How big they have gotten. Flashes appeared quickly. Fragments returned. Still, their names eluded me.

Another lapse in time has occurred. My apologies to anyone reading this. It has been at least several hours since I stopped writing momentarily. I have committed another sin in that void of time. One that I am afraid cannot be undone. I have damaged myself. I have damaged myself, irreconcilably. Not physically but via emotive and psychological means.

I have burned and vandalized several journals. Some are now nothing more than ash. Others have many pages torn out. I don't know what I have done to myself.

As one page was burning, I briefly saw the names of my children. I was filled with shame. I froze. I wanted desperately to reach into the flames to save the page, but I couldn't move an inch. I watched as the page curled and turned black before my eyes. An image drifted through my mind in that moment, of my kids running through a sprinkler in the backyard. They called for me to join. For a reason I have regretted ever since, I said no, maybe later. I don't know if later ever came. I don't regret burning the pages, but I do regret not playing with them on that day when I could, should, have.

Perhaps they are all better off without me. Dare I say something like that? Why torture my own family with my presence. My everlasting, horrific, curse of an existence.

Maybe, just maybe I am not only not needed in this life, but not wanted. I don't want to continue like this. I think, I may know, that perhaps I do want to die.

Chapter Three
November 3, 2020

I fear something is very wrong with what I am doing. Something is, not missing exactly, but wrong, unclean, definitely not right.

I was at the police station today. I was interrogated: my mind split open, my very self pulled apart at the seams. I fear my insanity is complete.

Let me start from the beginning, from where I last remember. The seats in the back of the cop car had been sticky, and smelled like a mixture of vomit and urine. I kept my mouth closed, as if that would keep the poison out.

The handcuffs felt cold even when we arrived at the station. I realized I was sweating profusely. My clothes clung to me. I struggled to adjust them, to no avail. The car door opened. I hadn't heard the policeman get out. A moment passed where the door remained opened. The officer leaned over and gestured for me to exit. He smiled at me warmly. He said it was alright and that I wasn't in trouble. I awkwardly moved along the seat and eventually staggered out of the car. My legs felt like jelly as they supported my weight once more.

A strange thought struck me as the officer led me into the station. I had recalled everything from the window until that point. I can't remember the last time I recalled such a great length of time.

The officer led me into a room with one table and a chair on either side. There was a two-way mirror on one wall. The space felt cold. I suddenly had the sensation that there was more to what had transpired today beyond my apparent suicide attempt. I wondered what had transpired prior to that event, and whether it was normal to handcuff people in my position?

The officer sat me down on one side of the table. He undid my handcuffs and placed them in front of me. He moved to sit opposite me. Several moments passed as we stared at each other. The man seemed familiar to me, but I couldn't place why. It was then I realized he wasn't even a true officer as I recall the word 'Trainee' written on his uniform.

He asked me what had happened today. What a ridiculous question to ask someone in my position. I can barely tell you the last several years; practically all my life is a mere fog to me; and this is your first question.

I remember saying that I couldn't answer accurately on any account.

He said he wanted to make it clear that I was not in any sort of trouble for what happened. He only wanted to talk with me.

The behavior of the officer was most intriguing, and I must admit the situation piqued my curiosity.

He said he had an admission to make. I remember him telling me that his mom recommended this visit, and that despite its obvious lunacy he should continue all the same.

"I'm afraid I don't follow," I told him, with a now profound level of interest. Part of me wished everything to stop, to not hear any more. However, I was glued to this man. I couldn't place why. Nothing else existed in this universe except what he was about to say next.

"I forgive you," I remember he said next.

His phrasing shocked me in a way I cannot describe. A pain shot up my neck. "What?" I remember saying quietly.

"Mom said to keep trying, so here I am," he said shakily. He wouldn't look me in the eye. I could tell he was crying slightly. It occurred to me that this may not have been the first time we had had this conversation.

"Trying to do what exactly?" This was my responses still perplexed.

"It's me dad, your son Brian."

All the world went still. The sound of the ticking clock on the wall stopped and all else froze in place. I didn't hear him correctly, I remember thinking. That's not possible. To have a son at all – let alone one who was grown, and training to be a police officer no less – was sheer and utter madness. For this to be real was for me to accept not just one potential truth, but a host of equally ridiculous implausibility's. For one, Ariadne would actually have to be my wife. Which in and of itself is problematic, because that can only be described as my con. A foolery, a forgery forced upon her. A punishment it would be to make her marry me and all my anchors and chains of burden. I could barely comprehend that absurdity.

But to now have a son out of all that, even more impossible still. However, it's not the same. No, it is very much a different thing altogether. A child could never be described as a con. A child is what all children are, especially in the eyes of a parent, and that is a miracle.

I had no proof whatsoever that this man in front of me, Brian, was in fact my son. He looked at me anxiously. He studied me, waiting for a response. My mind raced with a flurry of flashes that felt like memories, but they appeared fractured and went by too quickly to focus.

He told me that everything was ok. I didn't believe him.

I asked him how many times we had had this conversation in the past. He looked at me thoughtfully. He said we had this conversation nearly every day, but to not worry about such things. Again, I didn't believe him.

"Every day?" I asked without thinking. He smiled warmly at me and said yes. He conveyed it was a normal part of his day and that it typically didn't take long. He described me as a smart man, and that I caught on quick. That was the first compliment I can ever recall hearing. The thought nearly brought tears to my eyes. It was a casual statement, but it meant more than can be described here and now. Tears are manifesting themselves even now.

"I'm so sorry," I blurted out frantically. "I'm just so sorry to be the burden that I am. I've missed so much that cannot be replaced. I remember not picking you up from school. Every thought I have, every memory that occurs in the endless void of my mind, is of how disappointing I must be to anyone close to me."

Brian raised a hand to stop. He smiled again. "At no point in my entire life were you ever a disappointment. You were an amazing father. We all knew how hard every day was, and I won't lie that it was a challenge, but I only have happy memories from it all, dad." As he said this my body strained to stay seated. My whole being wanted to get up and hug him, my son, my boy. I always dreamt of having a son, but to see a grown man here, physically in front of me, saying he is my son. The feeling is, was, surreal.

This was my greatest forgery yet. The greatest, most inconceivable, betrayal of my mind. The con was that, for all this time, I hoped the only one who I could hurt was myself. The only one I could spite was the man I saw in the mirror. Except, it can't be. It can't be a forgery. How can I be so despicable, yet there be an innocent boy that became of it. Either my lies have created ever increasingly intricate fantasies, of which my exile to the deepest recesses of my mind is complete. Or I have been fundamentally wrong about something.

I was drifting again. I knew it, as I recognize it now. It was the start of losing track. I oftentimes could feel when things were starting to slip back into oblivion. Why struggle against something that felt so natural and complete. From there I would wake up: sometimes minutes, sometimes days, later. However, this time was different. I surprise myself even now that I can articulate this. What remains of these journals is fractured, burnt in some places. A residual, lingering feeling persisted, continues to persist: that someone is torturing me with these journals. Like solving a puzzle with half the pieces missing.

Brian started describing various memories of his. He chronicled several times I went to his baseball games. He told me how I was always wearing his jersey, cheering him on. I took meticulous care of the jersey he would tell me. It hung on the door of my home office for years. A proud reminder of his son's success. We would talk those evenings after the game discusses the plays. A fire of excitement in our eyes. The memories filled me with a refreshment of hope. He then told me how currently I would often refuse to be brought up to speed on most things in order to focus on the present. I often would say how precious minutes were to me. These revelations seemed at odds with one another. Perhaps it was out of a small sense of futility to not go over the same memories endlessly. Subconsciously, I must have kept him from this.

He jumped to his high school graduation. He took out a small picture from his wallet and handed it across the table. I felt my hand vibrate touching the old photo. It was the first time I can recall seeing myself. As hard as I struggled I could recall no other time when I had seen myself. I studied myself for what felt like a long while. My features seemed foreign to me, but what I can remember now was that I was smiling, and that is what matters. In the photo there was a man, a woman, and two teenagers. A boy and a girl. The boy, Brian, was in full graduation attire. I opened my mouth to ask of the girl.

It's gone. It was there, clear as day. The picture. He said her name. Ariadne, Brian, me, and her. Think. If I try and write it, it will come.

I was doing so well. It was there. It was there, I know it. If someone, anyone else ever reads this. Write her name here. Right here. Then I can remember her. She had her mother's eyes. I know that. They were hers.

As I struggled to retain what little fragment there was in my depleted mind, the door of the room swung in. A large man in uniform entered stiffly. Brian shot up from his chair, speaking to the officer and getting between him and myself. The two men argued about something I couldn't make out. Their voices sounded muffled as my mind drifted between remnants of the fading photograph and thoughts of where Ariadne was at that moment. After finding out I had a family, I somehow felt even more alone than I did earlier today.

Before I could fully return to the present, the large man was in the process of putting the handcuffs back on my wrists. Brian lunged forward to stop him, but the man forced the cuffs on me. Once the cuffs clicked into place he dragged me to my feet. My son's face was red with anger. He stressed that I didn't mean to do what I did. The statement echoed over and over again. The large man tried to force me through the door out into the hall. I pulled and twisted my hands free of his grasp. The man turned, a surprised expression on his face, and began to berate me, trying once again to grab my hands. I found myself breaking into a run, passing him, and he took off down the hall in pursuit. Brian was after me as well, demanding for me to stop. I heard him plead for me to not make it worse for myself.

Several officers came out of nowhere and tackled me off my feet. I hit the floor with such force that I heard several cracks from within my body. I struggled to move, but was kept in place.

Amongst the many voices all talking over one another, I could feel the darkness creeping back into my mind. I knew what was coming. Soon it would be tomorrow, or next week, or next year. It was different every time. Except, this time the old familiar feeling of sadness wasn't there. It wasn't an emptiness, or as if something were missing. It was rather, or more explicitly, that something has been added back in. It wasn't just that Ariadne was real, but even more than that. The one other thing that was true, was that, I have a son.

Chapter Four
November 4, 2020

Something miraculous is happening to me. I remember something; something more than just today. The last two days, in fact, are there. They are here, in my mind. I know and fear it will not last. But - for the time I have with these precious, irreplaceable, fragile memories - I will savor them until there is nothing left.

Yesterday, I found out that I have a son. I know that my joy in meeting him was met by his profound, and rightly deserved, heartbreak. My son is not a boy, he is a man. The level of sadness I felt yesterday is not even comparable to depths of the mourning I have now, but in the time I had with him yesterday it was happiness. Pure, crystalline, and completely free of sorrow.

Today was another gauntlet of emotion, perhaps even more of a blow to the heart than meeting my grown son.

Today, I met my daughter.

Let me start from the beginning.

I found myself waking up in a hospital bed. My body ached and moaned from strain, and I looked down to find small bruises down my arms. The skin was irritated somehow. It didn't occur to me how it happened. Even now, I am not too sure of the details. I lifted my arms to feel my face, but only one followed my command. My left wrist was handcuffed to the bed. The skin under the cuff was raw from strain. I must have resisted at some point, though when I cannot recall.

Although I remember so much from the last two days, last night still seems to be gone. The bright memory of my son filled my heart once again, warming me. Despite the burden that I am on the world, at least I made something of it, my dear boy.

It is a parent's job to sacrifice their children, so to speak, to the world once they are old enough to carry their own responsibility. Such is the cycle of life. Apparently, even a broken cycle can still produce a great child; though I don't know to what extent I even helped. It may have been, and mostly likely was, all Ariadne.

Three women with student nametags came into the room and huddled together at the end of the bed as an older woman nurse circled them to come around by the window to my left. She rattled off information that indicated she was talking about me, the students wrote hastily to keep up.

I stared at the window, waiting for the urge to jump to resurface. But no desire came in that regard. The postulation of immediately equating the window to a desire to want to jump is still worrisome. I sense I am still a danger to myself, and that I have a long way to go. And someone else must have put that together, hence my being cuffed to the bed.

The nurse remained silent as she studied me then her clipboard. How dispassionate she seemed. I don't recall her making eye contact with me at any point. How small you can be made to feel, how insignificant. In my head I screamed at her to look at me, but my lips remained closed. I don't know why I remained silent. After all, I had nothing to lose.

She murmured several things, darting glances over the clipboard at me. Some of the students listened to her intently. The nurse scribbled some notes, then got up and left without a word more. The pack of students turned, staying on her heels as they too funneled out the door. One student paused and remained, staring at me with a meek expression on her face. She stood there, looking frightened, yet still took a few shaky steps closer.

"Hello," I said awkwardly. I remember gesturing for her to sit by the window. She let out a small laugh and obliged.

For a moment we studied at each other as if trying to recollect an old acquaintance. "Why am I handcuffed?" I asked finally. I meant to say something friendlier, but couldn't help myself. "Oh that," she said with kindness in her voice. "It was just a misunderstanding. I'm sure they will take those off soon. Brian said it wouldn't be long." The name didn't register. "Who is that?" I asked sharply.

"One of the officers," she said, trailing off. Her face looked defeated. Suddenly the memories of yesterday flashed through my mind and the name struck me like a blow to the temple. "My son!" I said loudly. "Brian is my son." The outburst caught the poor girl off guard, but a bright smile suddenly appeared across her face. "Yes," she replied. "Yes, yes, that's right." She wiped a small tear from her eye as she readjusted herself on the chair. "You remember," she said cheerfully, taking my hand. "You're back," she said, looking at me through a beaming smile of relief.

"I am," I said warmly. "So you must be my princess." She let out a small giggle wiping away another tear. "My name is Kristin."

The joy I felt in that moment was almost indescribable. Several memories washed over me as partial pieces of the puzzle were added to the board. How could I have missed so much; so many moments that were so worth remembering. So much of my journals are dedicated to the moments that give the darkness within me reason enough to spread, to cast an ever-increasing shadow upon my life. Before me now is evidence, proof from the mouth of my own daughter saying otherwise.

Perhaps there is more light to my reality than I am aware of. To have produced not just one, but two beautiful children, and to have a wife who, despite the difficulties, still remains by my side. Maybe I am not all monster, like I often think I am in these pages. These journals harbor my secrets, but the greatest secret they may hold is the truth that I may yet be a good man.

A sensation came over me then, that this may all be temporary. Had I had moments of clarity like this before? Scanning through some vandalized journals now it's hard to tell. I knew in that moment not to waste precious time.

"So you're a nursing student?" I asked cautiously, not knowing if I had possibly asked that question of her numerous times in the past. "Yes," she answered, with no hint of frustration on her face. She seemed glad to be talking to me. I searched her features for any trace of a lie - that would tell me she in fact loathed me like I suspected everyone must - but still, nothing.

"Have I asked that before?" I asked, unable to control myself. "Don't dwell on any of that." Her answer was both quick and reassuring. "Just stay with the now." She stroked my wrist with her hand. "How old are you?" I asked, struggling to stifle the myriad questions I wanted to put to my precious girl. "It doesn't matter dad. I'm grown. I am attending nursing school, and I attend classes and work here now. I wanted to stay close to home to help out. To help Mom."

"With me," I said sullenly. "No, it's not like that," she added quickly. "You're too hard on yourself dad. You know you visited me at school nearly every week. Mom drove you. We would eat lunch together and talk about everything really."

That's hard to believe, I remember thinking, uncertain whether I only thought that, or said it aloud. Nevertheless, she could tell what had occurred to me. "You see, Dad, and I know you may not remember this, but as a family we made a deal, that we would all stick together. That it was the only way to not let this beat us. We're a team, and we all love you."

She said a decision was made, one that was not made lightly. It would be to not just fill me in on what was important, but to also not tell me certain things. That is to say, that a sort of fantasy was to be created around me. Now, I must confess as she told me this that I was sick with guilt. Suddenly, it occurred to me how much I may have missed. I thought how much was skipped, lost, altered, or outright misled. My thoughts turned to the missing pages in my journals. Perhaps it was not me that tore out those pages. Maybe it was my own family. Protecting, insulating me, not just from the outside world, but from myself.

Would my family, my loved ones, arrive at this conclusion - this final solution - without my input? Did they seek to pull a sort of wool over my eyes, or did they in fact consult me?

I dread to think whether it was me myself who came up with this illusionary facade? I'll admit the thought doesn't seem that much of a stretch There isn't much reason for a hard truth to dampen the euphoria of a lie.

"Was it my idea?". I couldn't bring myself to look her in the eye as I spoke. "Partly," she said, with a brightness in her voice. "It wasn't to trick you, I assure you. It was to not burden you with things that truly did not matter."

"Yes," I said again. Thinking on it, I suppose that makes sense to some degree. In the brief moments that I am lucid and able to focus on anything for just a few minutes, why would I spend it reminding myself of all that is missed. "Yes, that makes sense," I said to her more confidently.

"How much time do I have?" I asked, a little more urgently. I felt a darkness creeping into the back of my mind. "It's hard to say," she said, gripping my hand tighter. "Maybe minutes, maybe a few hours. Don't focus on that. What would you like to discuss?" The tone of her voice had brightened even more, still there was a desperation in her voice I couldn't quite quantify. I trusted her implicitly to not take advantage of me in that situation.

My mind drifted to what felt like an old memory of Ariadne screaming. What she was screaming about was gone. It was all blurred, blended. All I knew was that she had seized the opportunity to say what she truly felt. Her therapy, as I might soon begin to describe it. Her release, and mine as well I suppose. It was a moment I partly remember, from when the foundation of deceit did not exist.

Some time passed - maybe a moment, or a few minutes - when my mind snapped back to the present. My mouth moved to speak without thought.

"Are you married?" I asked, plucking one of the thousand questions from the queue in my mind. She laughed. She turned her head, realizing how loud she was, responding to the abruptness of the question. "No, no not yet," she said, tempering herself.

"Oh.". I was worried that was something I had missed. As the moment of levity wore off, a sudden and deliberate dark notion surfaced within me.

"You said you all came to an agreement on what to tell me. Was there something that brought on such an agreement? What did I do or not do? Or rather, what was something you wouldn't tell me?" I asked slowly. I stared and studied her carefully. My stomach turned as I awaited the reply.

"I don't want to tell you any of that dad," she said, placing her other hand on mine.

"Please, I know it won't matter anyway, but I'd like to know something that is real. So much is undiscernible in my mind. Everything is a mix of reality and fiction. I'd like to know something that is true in its incompleteness. Would you do that for me please, as a favor." My words were tinged with desperation, and self-deprecation. I knew I was risking the long breath of rejuvenation that was my memory returning these past days, but I needed to know the dream, the fantasy it has been this far, was grounded in something resembling truth. I needed to know that good could bleed.

I could tell she wanted to cry. I didn't want to hurt her, yet something I said had inflicted something amounting to pain. Immediately, I had wanted to reach out to her, but I knew that doing so may have kept her from continuing.

"There was a day, many years ago," she started, sitting upright in her chair. Her face seemed drained of color as she hesitated. Her eyes drifted off , glimpsing into that dark recess of her mind where the truth must have been hidden. "You were having a particularly bad stretch where you were stuck," she continued coldly. "You were stuck on the idea that we were all strangers to you. Strangers that at first were harmless, but as time progressed became something of a threat. The conclusion you reached was that you wanted to run away. As far as possible, you wanted to escape. One night, you left. A bag was packed and you called a taxi to take you to the airport. It was the sound of the car driving off that finally woke mom. She got the rest of us up and we took off after you. It was cold out and Mom couldn't stop crying. None of us could. None of us spoke, but the thought that we may never see you again was there. I dare say it was the saddest moment of my life."

Kristin pulled her hand away from mine to wipe her eyes.

"Go on," I encouraged, needing to hear the rest. "Please.". My voice was hoarse with desperation.

"When we got to the airport -" she continued with her head low "- we left the car at the drop-off spot. I think Mom left the keys in the ignition. We were all in such a state that we weren't thinking clearly. We ran, we ran so hurriedly through the crowd of people. So many faces, all going their separate ways. Brian and I had thought it futile to try and find you, but Mom was so filled with hope. I'm ashamed for giving up that hope. I'll be sorry for that for the rest of my days."

"By some miracle we caught up with you at security. You didn't see us standing there; but there you were. I thought for sure that Mom would run to you, but she hesitated. Brian started to, but Mom stopped him. Look at him, she had said to us. Just look. The three of us stared as you were calmly putting your bags through the scanner and going through TSA, as if nothing were wrong in the world. I'll never forget it, but you were happy, Dad."

I reached out my hand to Kristin, and she placed hers back in mine. I smiled at her and told her it was ok. "I forgive you", I remember saying to her. "It's ok. You don't have to feel guilty for any of that."

"No," she said, pulling her hand back once again. "I'm not at the part yet where I feel most ashamed.

"While we stood there watching, Mom said something; something that sickens me even now to think about. While we stood there, Mom told us to look at how happy you were. Brian and I agreed that we hadn't seen you that happy in so long. She asked us if it would be so bad to leave you like that. I remember staring at her in horror, in absolute horror, at her suggestion. 'We can't do that,' I said to her, starting to step back. 'It's inhuman, that's our dad.'

"I must confess, dad, it was horrid, absolutely nightmarish, for Mom to suggest such a thing. It is perhaps the single greatest regret in my life that I didn't strike down her notion that instant. I should have - I would have, had I been stronger, been better than I wanted to. I should have been a better daughter. But I wasn't. Not then, not in that despicable moment. In that moment I was a monster, an idiot, a survivalist. I know that's an abysmal reason to give, especially now, especially to you, but that is the truth. That is the whole wretched truth of it. I know you must hate me hearing this. You must want to disown me, your own daughter, but I would take it. I deserve it. I do. I know I don't deserve anything better.

"Anyway, Mom just looked at me after not having even made a lowly attempt at a rebuttal, simply said nothing. I remember she looked to Brian, who seemed in a daze trying to contemplate his answer. He just looked at you, Dad, at the gate. You were still smiling, talking to some people next to you in line. We had no doubt in our minds that you were describing how you were on your way to see your family. "

Kristin dropped her face into her hands and sobbed. I remember feeling nothing just then. My heart wanted to fill up with condemnation, but I was uncertain whether that was appropriate. How could I hate them for being human? Is it such a sin to want the best for someone, even if it was counterintuitive to one's own desires? They loved me. I am sure of that much at least. or at least as much as I am capable.

"What did you do?" I asked. She raised her head, almost shocked by the question.

"Yes, I think I'd like to know," I asked again.

"We let you get on the plane, if you must know. There, ok, I said it. Is that what you wanted to know? How unkind, how cruel we were." She cried harder at the second admission.

"No, no, I don't mean that at all. I thank you for what you did, sincerely I do." I leaned forward in the bed to take up her hands once more. "It was a kind thing you did for me, to let me go. I know it may not have seemed right, but for what it's worth, it was."

"What?" she said, struggling to articulate her disorganized thoughts.

"Yes, it's ok," I said, smiling at her. My lovely girl. "I know you don't understand why I'm saying this. I know you must expect my anger or frustration. It's more than likely we have had this exact conversation in that past."

"We haven't," she said, quickly interrupting me.

"Something is happening these past few days Kristin. A clarity has befallen me. One I hope will last, as long as it can, because it has allowed me to think of what actually matters. It's a question - one that occurred to me recently - that is guiding all of this for me. My aim is to cherish what I have, instead of what I missed. That is the basis of the question. The question itself is far simpler. What would I rather do: be spiteful, and hateful, of all that is working against me; or enjoy, and be grateful for all that represents the positive in my life, which is my family. You, Brian, and mom. It's a simple question, one that is exceedingly easy to answer. However, countless years have robbed me of the basis of that question. My intention is to never focus on what was robbed from me ever again. So far as I can, only what I love shall occupy my attention. It is with that, I forgive you. I forgive, not just that action, but any that you feel shame for. I intend to forgive you all, if my clarity permits me. This disease is a plague on our family. As much as I am the sufferer, the greatest burden was placed upon you three. My sympathy for you three could not be deeper. You are allowed to get frustrated; not just at the situation, but at me as well. I cannot condemn you for that, ever. If, in your attempts to make things better for yourselves and me, you chose to create a kind of fantasy for me, I will embrace it. Is it a lie? Maybe, but if it leads to our happiness, who can fault that? You all have stayed by my side this long. What else can I do, except say thank you."

Kristin was silent, staring at me intently. The tears stopped, but her eyes remained red. She leaned forward and kissed my forehead gently. "I missed you," she said softly.

"I missed you too," I said. My heart ached with love in that moment. A warmth came over me as I suddenly felt drowsy. The medicine I must have been on was taking effect. I gripped Kristin's hand tightly as my nerves caused my hands to tremble.

"Will you still be here when I wake up?" I asked with a crack in my voice. "I'm scared that I may not remember any of this when I do. So much came back just now, I don't want to lose it."

Kristin placed her hand alongside my face. "Even if you don't remember," she said. "It doesn't make it mean any less. Love you Dad."

Her words echoed in my mind as all drifted to black. It wasn't a coldness I felt, but a warmth that I can only describe as hope.

Chapter Five

February 18, 1990

My first entry. My doctor said I should commence now. She said I should begin writing every thought down and recapping everything at the end of each day.

So here I am, writing my diary. I was supposed to start weeks ago, but I have more important matters to attend to. So childish it is to write in a diary. I feel as if I am a teenage girl or something. I shouldn't have written that. Perhaps I'll tear out this page and begin again. In a few months, I could probably forget I ever did that.

I am stalling again. Let me embark with my session today.

"Where should I initiate?" I remember saying shortly after we sat down.

"We can start however you like, but it is important to start. You've stalled the last three sessions," she said, sitting in her chair opposite me. Her voice commanded the room. Immediately I found a sense of respect for her. As much as I contested the very idea of having to see a shrink, I must admit she was what I needed all along, a dose of reality. The space didn't feel like a doctor' office. She must have been doing well for herself to operate a shrink's practice out of her home.

I say shrink, which must sound and drip with some disrespect, but I assure you it is only a superficial condemnation.

I waited for that telling, piercing gaze I had grown accustomed to as of late. When most people hear I have a memory disease the usual chuckles follow, then it's followed up by confusion, and then finally judgement. Always in that order. As I am in the early stages it's usually regarded as an excuse. No one has yet to take me seriously, even Ariadne. A tinge of anxiety hit me as the thought of my impending wedding day came to my mind. What if she calls it off? How even more hopeless all would become.

"I proposed to my partner Ariadne two months ago, about two weeks prior to my diagnosis. Does that make me an evil man?" I asked honestly.

"Do you feel evil for having said it? Perfectly natural to feel guilty now. I wont lie to you, it will be a difficult road," she said calmly. Her voice was soothing in its bluntness. It surprised me.

Whereas I had shocked myself with the corruptness of my thoughts; asking whether I was an evil man. Ariadne and I had been in love for about three years, an engagement was inevitable. Last night we got stuck in the rain in the city. We ran to find cover, but it was too late. She threatened to chase me and give me a hug in all her wet clothes. For a moment, we were two kids in love again. The innocence of the moment was timeless. She laughed in the rain. I hope to always remember that.

"Love is a powerful thing. You shouldn't fear it. You can't let fear consume you. Don't let it push your loved ones away. Don't let it make you resentful." Her words were like a chisel to my mind. I remember, I began reciting those words in my head as I sat there on her couch. They were my lifeline, my prayer. They were my chance at normalcy.

She must have sensed my apprehension to continue. Her eyes looked through me to my core. How vulnerable I felt then.

Still, I remembered what Ariadne said about detailing as much as possible now. Establish a base, a mental frame of reference, she had said, urging me to see this psychologist.

Humility can be just as vile and wretched as arrogance. I must concede that someday these words will be all I have. So they must be solid, unyielding.

"Let's talk about what lies ahead of you, your future. Tell me what you hope to achieve in time," she said, smiling warmly. "What do you want from life?"

The thought absolutely terrified me. All my mind could focus on was what would be lost in time. People, faces, actions, thoughts: all of it gone, lost.

She seemed to sense where my mind was leading me.

"Focus, don't let your mind drift again. Be in the room. You have to practice." she said, reassuringly.

"I, want a family," I blurted out. The statement surprised even me. "No, I didn't mean that exactly. I, I, I'll start again."

"Your there, don't lose that train of thought. Focus. Now continue," she said, leaning forward with sincerity.

"What I mean to say is this." I remember I paused for what felt like a long while. A reason has been boiling up within me that was near a breaking point.

"There are things I want out of life. Things that I need to have happen. The first is simply that I want to face the future. Now, I am fearful of it. I cower at the mere contemplation of even five minutes from now. I am living with the ever-present horror of the knowledge that even two seconds from now my entire reality could be wiped out of existence. Do you have any idea of the insanity behind something like that?"

My outburst surprised me yet again. The anger built within me in that moment as the words spilled out of my mouth uncontrollably. The release felt good. It felt right.

"I wish more than anything I could muster the strength to not have that fear. Even if that pride was a delusion, a lie built on nothing but false conviction, I'll take it. I'll take it every day if possible. I want to be able to enjoy a moment without the ceaseless possibility of the inevitably of nothingness."

I remember my hand started shaking. The truth was finally out, finally free.

"I want to remember Ariadne. I want to remember that she is here. The prospect of her imminent disappearance sickens me. I need her, I need her next to me, guiding me. If I could only have one person in the world it would be her. I know the day will come that she will still be there, but I won't remember her. I want to spare her from that, but how can I. How can I do that? It's selfish to want to keep her close after that, knowing I can never reciprocate. I may not be a monster on a lot of things, but on that I am the most horrid."

I felt lightheaded as I continued my outpouring of honesty.

"I want to keep a record of my days. I need them. I need them whole. Not because of making note of each and every tiny, minute action, but to chronicle that I am trying to be a better man. When the day comes that I am useless to myself in terms of remembering, these journals will be all I have. So they must be correct. I need them, to know how I was the day before. It will be the only way to be better the next day. To be who I want to be, not just who I am now."

"To use these notes is to ensure I am using my time here to bring purpose to not only myself, but to bring meaning to it all. Right now, I have no aim." A pit formed in my throat. I wanted to deny that admission. It couldn't be true. It isn't. I must write that it isn't. It is not. I have aim.

"No, that's not right. I have aim. I do." I remember staring at her as I spoke. My eyes searched desperately for a response, but she remained still in her chair with a hopeful look in her eyes. I was saying what she wanted I think.

"My aim is for my family, my future family. Kids, if we have kids. We will have kids. I must teach them to be better, better than me." Again, my voice stopped.

"Yes, continue," she said finally. Her pen had left the paper. The only noise in the room was the ticking of the clock. How arrogant the sound of a clock is: incessantly reminding us that we are one second closer to our demise than we were before.

"But there are things I fear, things that I fear will get in the way of my aim. Hindrances, blockades. Betrayals: not just by others, but myself." My body felt frozen, stuck on the words. My throat clenched, almost choking on the very thoughts crossing my mind.

"Let's try and stay on the good, you tend to wander into yourself too much. You succumb to your own nihilism easily. This is what you must face if you are to survive," she said, leaning further forward in her chair. She placed the notepad and pen on the side table next to her. She looked at me with intent.

"There appear to be many people around you that love you. There are no hurdles there as far as I can tell, no blockades as you say. There is nothing to fear. Let that be your guide while its there."

Her words did little to quell the anxiety within me. "Surrounded by people that love me, but for how long will I know that? How long will I retain the necessary information needed to discern that? Soon all will be an endless stream of discovery, of a never-ending investigation into the otherwise mundane. I will be surrounded by people, yet lonelier than I can ever describe. A person could be right next to me physically, but worlds away in connection. It's a dreadful thought, and yet soon to be my entire reality." My thoughts drifted to even earlier that morning, and Ariadne's profile next to me in bed. She slept so peacefully. Her dark brown hair stood out against the white pillow. I drank in that moment, not knowing when I would be present enough to savor it again. The thought made me want to scream at the world.

"That will be a challenge, yes. But that is when you must trust yourself. Trust that there are people around you, maybe not to trust as much as you want, but at least you can know there is someone there to assist. It's a difficult thing to be vulnerable, to let what will be a 'stranger' in, but it is necessary to try. That will be all you have which is why you must start writing now. You have already wasted weeks." She stared at me with a concerned shine in her eyes. She looked on the verge of tears. They would be tears of pity I know. I have seen them before.

"How can I trust, especially myself? I will write in my journal, capturing a fraction of the day. Plus it's in my own hand, couldn't I delude myself and say anything? There's no proof in any of this. All of this could be made up. Ariadne, friends, anyone could all be in my head, delusions, forgeries, lies. Of what use am I to myself if that is true? My God, what is true anymore? It's all just lies upon lies." I remember raising my hand at that point and noticing it was shaking.

"Trusting yourself will be the hardest part of all this," she replied, picking up her notepad once more and writing at speed. "You see, all there is, and all that exists in your own mind is two things. There is identity and there is trust. One does not exist without the other. And it must be in that order only. You must know who you are at all times in order to trust your own instincts. Without that, without a sense of self, how can you know who to trust, and why? It is an ever -resent challenge we all must face. Except with you, what we are here to work out is your identity. Your baseline. For everyone else it's memory. Memory is how you know where you have been, and you use that in order to build towards the future, a better self. For you, we have to manifest those things tangibly first, then the rest follows. Unfortunately, no one else can do this for you. There is only yourself, and what you translate as words on the page. That must be accurate; for it will be all you have, despite the help you receive. The stakes could not be higher, because if something is inaccurate, if you do lie to yourself, your entire perception will be so skewed, so corrupted, you may never find your way back again. What worse fate could you bring upon yourself by losing track of whether you can trust yourself?" She did not look up from the page once as she spoke. At its core, it was a sort of sermon, designed to appeal to my better self. Part of me resented her for her intellect. I wanted to reprimand her for her arrogance of knowledge, and to chide her for treating me like an idiot, a fool. However, there was no fallacy committed so far as I could tell.

"But I don't trust myself now." The admission filled me with shame.

"It's clear you don't. At least you can admit it. You are almost over your denial. During your first session, you maintained there was nothing wrong with you. You demanded to be left alone. To be exiled from everything and everyone. You have come a long way. You should be proud of that step, but there are many steps left ahead. But together we will get there." she added with a smile.

"I'm afraid my mind is plagued by contradictions these days. On one hand I don't feel particularly proud of anything, but on another if Ariadne actually marries me then I will be the happiest man alive. I don't think I'm able to reconcile those two things."

I remember in that moment I couldn't picture Ariadne's face. I strained to picture even a photograph of her in my mind. It was blurred. A sensation of panic engulfed me. As the seconds ticked by in all their mockery, still nothing surfaced. After nearly five minutes of silence it appeared. Suddenly I could see Ariadne in my mind, in all her beauty. My heart had been racing. My body was awash with anxiety. My breathing had quickened. For a moment I thought she was gone forever.

"Where were you just now?" she asked, as it became apparent to me how much time had elapsed.

"I, I couldn't recall Ariadne's face just now. That's something else that terrifies me, trusting myself aside. How am I to remember something like her face?"

"I'm afraid the burden of that may not be in your hands. When I spoke with Ariadne in my last session with her she made commitments to stay by your side, no matter the struggles, to remind you of all she can. I impressed the level of sacrifice needed to keep a promise such as that, and she agreed. She is a remarkably strong-willed woman, and in my field on top of that. However, I understand how difficult it can be to have a spouse as a patient. When she reached out, I was happy to help. You're very lucky to have such a supportive and committed partner." She sat back in her chair, visibly more relaxed. She closed her journal and returned it to the side table.

The pit in my stomach returned once again thinking of my upcoming proposal. A certain apprehension took hold of me. I loved her too much to separate the selfish need for help with my genuine desire to have her in my life. That was the root of the contradiction within me. I knew I could not stay in this hellish state of limbo. I could no longer avoid the consequences of evading reality. A choice would have to be made in order to move forward. Despite the uncertainty of the future I knew my life would be brighter with Ariadne in it. I knew I had to make the most daring step of trust I could with not only myself, but her as well.

"I think I have my answer, of what I will do," I said, attempting a smile back at the doctor.

"What is that?" She said brightly.

"I've decided I won't push her away, I will marry Ariadne."

Chapter Six

November 24, 2020

I am a happy man. Where before me laid nothing but darkness, ahead of me I finally see a light.

I feel like my old self again. How many decades it has been since I have had this much clarity. I know it won't last, but for now it is bliss. It is riding atop a wave in the sunset. All the colors and textures of existence are on full display. Everything is in slow motion as my whole body and senses strive to suck every drop, vacuum every crumb, of happiness out of life.

The house was full of voices. I could hear Brian and Kristin talking in the living room. Ariadne was helping me cook dinner. We're going to eat dinner again, as a family. Together. Together is how we survive, it's how all this makes sense.

A person can survive on their own. Objectively, that is possible. A person can procure all that is needed for sustenance and survive practically. But, to truly be happy, to find meaning, to find what we as humans need for our very souls, is connection. What connection is more needed, more important than the connection of family?

Ariadne smiled at me as we worked side by side in the kitchen. Thoughts drifted by, of what Kristin had said the other day about what was told to me and what wasn't. Were there days when this scene was considered normal, or was this a rarity? It's difficult to say. Amongst my never-ending research through the partially burned remains of my journals, I have yet to discover any mention of dinners together. It is entirely possible this is the first time we had ever done this as a family. If that is the case, as it more or less could be, then are these smiles real, or another illusion.

I must set that notion aside. I must table it for another time. Of what use is it to suspect anything? It will not bring me even one iota of happiness, or offer any comfort of any kind to know that a lie is even taking place.

My hands move, stirring the vegetables crackling in the pan. Hot oil splatters hit my wrist, reminding me of the now, the present, the real.

But, something did happen the other day. I sense it, I know it somehow. It's there: a splinter, a shred, a miniscule hint of doubt lurking in my shell of my brain. Something Kristin said. I remember asking her earlier today about our conversation in the hospital. There was a conversation, there were words exchanged, yet the details of that event are somewhat fuzzy. I asked her to elaborate on what we spoke about. She said it was mostly pleasantries and how certain things were kept from me. That statement caught my attention instantly. I pressed her for more intricacies, but she insisted that was the extent of it. She said that I grew tired and fell asleep before she left me to my rest. I believed her, I think I still do, but how yet to be certain.

There is something there, beyond what was said. Something uncomfortable, something resembling truth.

Again, I am at the intersection of inherent contradictions that define my life. Have I, or rather has someone else, been rewriting my own past, or is what I have been documenting accurate? A stray memory came from the word trust. Yes, I remember having a conversation like that at one point about trust, and more specifically trusting myself. I must make a decision: either to continue to entertain notions of self-deception, or to trust that things are ok, normal, and without suspicion. I understand the truth is somewhere in the middle, but for the present moment I must choose a side. For now, seeing my family together, remembering who they are, the choice is clear. I must trust the immediacy of now, for that is all I have.

We gathered around the table and sat. Several minutes passed during which no one said anything. Kristin's eyes were filled with tears, but not ones of sadness.

"How was work, dear?" Ariadne asked Brian casually. The simplicity of the question, its innocent brightness, surprised me. Some part of me waited for the inevitable addressing of the elephant in the room, which was me. I waited for the tears, the apologies, the promises, and so on. None came. It seemed all were committed to having as normal a time as possible. Whether it was out of innocence, guilt, or deceit, it did not matter. I knew I had a choice to make right then. To let this charade or truth - whatever it was - continue, or to fight for what was left of my dignity and call their bluff.

The truth was, and is, that I was tired of fighting this thing in my head, this doubt. And so the decision seemed clear enough to me. I'd rather be happy and enjoy life with the people right here in front of me. There was no need to question what was so blatantly obvious. I love my family, and they love me.

Brian launched into a story about a case he was working on. We all stared in captivation. It was a burglary. A classic case. No one was injured, but the clues were few and far between. He took us through how he worked the case and showed a great level of attention to detail in his work. Everyone asked questions here and there, me included. There were moments of laughter all around.

Kristin picked up on something Brian said and started
in on a story of her own. There were no tears left in
her eyes then. Only smiles were present at the table.
Sounds of chairs shuffling and forks on the plates
filled the background. To anyone else the scene
would be commonplace, rudimentary even, but it was
symbolic of something else entirely. It was affirmation
of a goal realized. A milestone of a completed race.
Countless years had gone by, the entirety of my
children's lives came and went, with nothing to show
for it. But, now, just for now only, it's all here. I
couldn't shake the smile from my face even if I
wanted to, and I don't.

I found Ariadne had been holding my hand for some
time. Her hand gently squeezed mine. Her skin was
soft, reassuring and safe.

Kristin's story somehow got onto the topic of a time
when the family was ice skating. More laughter came
from everyone. Suddenly a thought occurred to me.
"Remember when you skated right into that
policeman and knocked him clean over?" I asked
confidently. The question silenced the table.
Everyone looked at me, in sheer surprise. I quickly
felt embarrassed for having said anything.

"But dad, you can't talk!" said Kristin. "Like two seconds later you skated into a wall." A few more seconds of silenced passed before we all erupted in laughter. My cheeks hurt before long. We were all lost in a moment of bliss, as all that had come before was gone.

I could see all that I had wanted from the very start right in front of me. Everything since the beginning of my affliction, perfectly in order. I could see my parents on my sixth birthday placing the cake in front of me. I could feel the graduation tassel in my hand for college. I could feel Ariadne's lips as we kissed for the first time. I could hear each of my children's cries as they were born. Every memory hit me like a gentle wave, reminding me of the single most important thing memories exist to do. To remind us, that despite everything that has happened, is happening, and will happen - that despite anything that may occur - all will be ok. That we are ok.

I remember. I have a wife. Her name is Ariadne. I remember her in all her beauty and kindness. Our hands, touching for the first time, as I hand her the coat that she dropped on the sidewalk, that day in the rain. The lump in my throat as I dared ask her name. Our date by the ocean appeared. The name of the place escapes me, but the feeling is still there, and that's what matters.

I have a son, Brian, my brave boy. I remember holding you for the first time. Your tiny hands and feet. Even then I was so proud of you and the man you would grow to be. I remember your wedding day, you were so handsome in your tux. I remember I tied your bowtie, the agonizing trickiness of those blasted things.

I have a daughter, Kristin, my princess. You are my light. I remember seeing you off on the first day of school. You turned around to wave at me so many times. I don't think you waved any fewer than four times each day that week. I am proud you want to become a nurse, so that you may spread your love and compassion as far as it can go.

And I remember, me. As I write this, my identity - my sense of belonging, my purpose for being on this planet . . . my reason, my multiple reasons . . .my desire . . . to love and to grow and to be with my family - is back. And my name. Yes, my name. My name is what all names are, a gatekeeper of my very self. It is all that stands in front of our identities, and it is the first thing we put out into the world to connect with one another. The name that is the foundation for it all, and what encapsulates you. My name...is...

The End